P9-AQG-064

A HOLE IN THE ROAD

Jakki Wood

F

FRANCES LINCOLN
CHILDREN'S BOOKS

E WOOD
A hole in the road /
35000094643862
MAIN

There is a hole in the road. It needs a new surface.

Workers use a drill to break up the old one.

A backhoe loader is fitted with a big hammer.

This does the job faster.

A mini-excavator makes the hole bigger.

A digger scoops up the rubble.

The rubble is loaded into a dump truck.

Then it is taken away.

A tipper truck brings crushed stones.

The stones fill in the hole.

Hot asphalt arrives in a dump truck.

It is used to make the hard surface of the road.

A paver spreads the hot asphalt…

over the road surface.

A road roller squashes the asphalt flat.

Workers make sure it is really smooth.

A road sweeper cleans the new road...

ready for cars to use again.

11 08

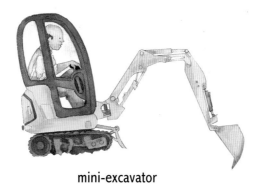

mini-excavator

For Isaac Harley Blann and Simeon Harding

A Hole in the Road copyright © Frances Lincoln Limited 2008
Text and illustrations copyright © Jakki Wood 2008

The right of Jakki Wood to be identified as the Author and Illustrator
of this work has been asserted by her in accordance with the
Copyright, Designs and Patents Act, 1988 (United Kingdom).

First published in Great Britain and in the USA in 2008 by
Frances Lincoln Children's Books, 4 Torriano Mews,
Torriano Avenue, London NW5 2RZ

www.franceslincoln.com

All rights reserved.
No part of this publication may be reproduced, stored in a retrieval system,
or transmitted, in any form, or by any means, electrical, mechanical, photocopying,
recording or otherwise without the prior written permission of the publisher
or a licence permitting restricted copying. In the United Kingdom
such licences are issued by the Copyright Licensing Agency,
Saffron House, 6-10 Kirby Street, London EC1N 8TS.

British Library Cataloguing in Publication Data available on request

ISBN: 978-1-84507-286-5

Printed in China

1 3 5 7 9 8 6 4 2